The Unofficial Book of Sci-Fi Haiku

Brandon Michaels

The Unofficial Book of Sci-Fi Haiku

X

@AuthorBMichaels

www.authorbrandonmichaels.com

Nudous Publishing, LLC

www.nudouspublishing.com
info@nudouspublishing.com

Paperback ISBN: 978-1-964793-97-9

Digital ISBN: 978-1-964793-09-2

This is a work of fiction. Names, characters, businesses, places, events, locales, and incidents are either the products of the author's imagination or used in a fictitious manner. Any resemblance to actual persons, living or dead, or actual events is purely coincidental.

Dedication

To those great creatives of sci-fi past and present, bequeathing us through their imagination and courage in the face of the unknown stories that were so much more than simple entertainment, they were lifelines, guiding lights, and inspirational sources. Through every adventure, every struggle between good and evil, every glimpse into what might be, your worlds have become a refuge from reality. A place where creativity knows no limit and hope never really dies. Among your spaceways, I have found not mere stories but hard-earned lessons in stubborn endurance, courage, and the dogged strength of the human spirit. Those worlds filled me with the courage to imagine, dream bigger, and see that even the least likely of heroes rise above the odds. Your works have breathed countless journeys into my mind and heart, shaping how I see the world in their remembrance that the future, however cloudy, has boundless possibilities. Thank you for creating worlds where anything is possible, where hope and endurance always have a way, and in which we can wander. There is always a path leading us home.

8/18/2024

Dear Readers,

Thank you for picking up this collection of haiku inspired by the many incredible sci-fi shows and movies that have fueled my imagination over the years. While iconic franchises like Star Wars and Star Trek are beloved by many (myself included), I chose to leave them out of this collection. With so much content already available celebrating those worlds, I wanted to highlight other stories and universes that also deserve attention.

In these haikus, I explore a range of often underappreciated works that have left a lasting impact on me. I hope this journey through diverse and unique sci-fi narratives brings you as much enjoyment as it brought me to create.

Thank you for joining me in this exploration of the stars and beyond.

Sincerely,

Brandon Michaels

Table of Contents

Babylon 5

Babylon station,
Port of call for refugees,
Smugglers, diplomats.

Centauri intrigue,
Shadows lurking in the void,
Babylon's saga.

Sinclair's leadership,
Whispers of the Grey Council,
Secrets in shadows.

Minbari reborn,
Delenn's bold transformation,
Linked in Valen's name.

Londo's tragic fate,

Centauri Republic's fall,

Babylon's sorrow.

Rangers on the edge,

Warrior caste's noble pledge,

Shon'kar Narn blood oath.

Psi Corps special ops,

Telepath revolution,

Alternative plan.

G'Kar's redemption,

Narn's struggle for freedom's light,

A Glimmer of hope.

Ivanova's strength,

Earth Alliance's complex,

Enemy's battle.

Vorlon enigma,

Kosh's long, cryptic past hidden,

Among the first ones.

Zathras speaks riddles,

Time's tapestry unravels,

Station four returns.

Rangers' protection,

Guardians of peace and light,

Virtuous fighters.

Shadow war erupts,
Vorlon and the Shadows clash,
The battle begins.

Sheridan's bold stance,
Babylon 5's last defense,
Outcome yet unknown.

Garibaldi's fall,
Security Chief betrayed,
Secret betrayal.

Morden's whispered deals,
Shadows manipulating,
Returns from the past.

Vir's rise to power,
Centauri Republic's change,
An evolution.

Lennier's sacrifice,
Unrequited love's despair,
A silent heartbreak.

Marcus in the dark,
Ranger's unyielding spirit,
Courage under fire.

Draal's hidden from view,
Great machine's ancient secrets,
Watching what to come.

The Rim's distant reach,
Outposts in uncharted space,
Galaxy's frontier.

Drazi colors swirl,
Purple and green in conflict,
Ivanova hurt.

Mimbari reborn,
Entwined with human stories,
Two souls join as one.

Kosh's perplexing words,
"In the beginning, the end,"
Hidden prophecy.

In Valen's name sworn,
Minbari honor and pride,
Following his path.

Babylon's silence,
Void echoes with lost whispers,
Memories remain.

Babylon's lanterns,
Guiding ships in the darkness,
Beacons of hope shine.

Narn homeworld freed,
G'Kar's prophecy fulfilled,
Rebuilding lost hope.

The Expanse

Leviathan Wakes,

Miller and Holden collide,

Stars whisper secrets.

Caliban's War cries,

Protomolecule unfolds,

Unknown danger lurks.

Abaddon's Gate calls,

Ring's mystery beckons all,

Gates to the unknown.

Cibola Burn's fire,

New worlds ablaze, conflicts rise,

Exploration's cost.

Tiamat's Wrath descends,

Final battle unfolds wide,

In the void, echoes.

Rocinante sails,

Heart of the Expanse's tale,

The heroic whispers.

Holden's moral path,

Amos, a gentle brute's soul,

Naomi's strength shines.

Protogen's dark plot,

Miller's noir detective quest,

Mystery unwinds.

Martian red allure,
Earther blue, Belters between,
Inequality.

Tycho Station hums,
Fred Johnson's bold gambit plays,
Belter's hope reborn.

Ilus, frontier,
In the shadow of the rings,
Colonists' struggle.

Corruption festers,
Earth and Mars play at their games,
Belter dreams endure.

Time's relentless march,

In the Expanse's vast sea,

Stories ebb and flow.

Holden's beacon shines,

Guiding through the cosmic dark,

Hope in the abyss.

Belter creole sings,

In the Belt's vast emptiness,

Songs of resistance.

Razorback's swift flight,

In the vacuum, whispers drift,

Echoes of the past.

Churn of Tycho's docks,
Ships depart, destinies shaped,
Choices in the void.

Dandelion's breeze,
Seeds of change in every arc,
Expanse unfurling.

Cant's haunting echoes,
Canterbury remembered,
Lost in the abyss.

Behemoth's grand hold,
Refuge for the lost and found,
Belter's floating home.

Screaming Firehawk,

Roci's crew, a family,

Bound by the unknown.

Rocinante's roar,

Thrusters blaze, through the unknown,

Legacy unfolds.

The pulses of the ring,

Mysterious pathways carved,

Fates entwined in space.

Pendulum's return,

Time's unyielding rhythm beats,

Expanse ever vast.

Voyage through the rings,
Exploration's endless quest,
Infinite unknowns.

Belter's anthem sung,
In the dark, rallying cry,
For freedom's embrace.

Ghosts of Eros haunt,
In the Belt, whispers linger,
Mystery unsolved.

Roci sails alone,
Through the silence of the void,
Legacy endures.

In the dark expanse,
Humanity's tale unfolds,
Echoes in the stars.

The Expanse's song,
Epic verses yet to be told,
In the cosmos vast.

Firefly

Serenity soars,

Captain's wit and crew's embrace,

Stars whisper their tales.

Browncoat rebels fight,

In the Black, they find their home,

Firefly's glow shines.

Shepherd's guiding words,

Mysterious past unfolds,

Faith in the void's grace.

River's mind untamed,

Dance of danger in her eyes,

Lost in psychic storm.

Jayne's cunning and brawn,

Mercenary heart concealed,

Hat hides true intent.

Kaylee's bright spirit,

Mechanical genius hums,

Engine's heartbeat sings.

Inara's grace blooms,

Companion's touch, silk and steel,

Love in every choice.

Wash's laughter echoes,

Pilot's whimsy in the stars,

Leaf on the wind soars.

Zoe's loyalty,

Warrior's strength in stillness,

Mal's partner in crime.

Malcolm leads with pride,

Rebel heart and captain's soul,

Firefly's journey.

Serenity's hum,

Journey through the black expanse,

Freedom in the stars.

Book's scriptures unfold,

Preacher with a hidden past,

Spirit in the void.

Alliance shadows,

Government's watchful eye looms,

Browncoats defy chains.

In the Core's embrace,

Injustice stains polished halls,

Outer worlds resist.

In the heart of space,

Echoes of a war untold,

Whispers in the wind.

Simon's sacrifice,

Doctor's love transcends the stars,

Healing in the void.

Companions dance free,
Inara's silk, allure blooms,
Love, fleeting glances.

Cunning hat's disguise,
Jayne's loyalty is unmasked,
Mercenary heart.

Wash's laughter rings loud,
Pilot's whimsy in the sky,
Leaf on the wind soars.

Miranda echos,
Secrets buried in the black,
Reapers' silent wail.

Saffron's fleeting lies,
Conwoman in a tight grip,
Heartache in the stars.

Cobb's betrayal stings,
Muddy past, uncertain trust,
Gunslinger's remorse.

Zoe's strength so strong,
Warrior's spirit shines through,
Mal's right hand is fierce.

In the Black they drift,
Firefly's crew, family,
Bound by loyalty.

River's mind untamed,
Whispers in the silent dark,
Dance of shadows wild.

Mal's moral compass,
Captain's heart in rugged form,
Leading through the storm.

Serenity's crew,
Outlaws in the cosmic sea,
Chasing freedom's light.

Jubal's dark pursuit,
Bounty hunter on their trail,
Danger in the void.

Haven in the stars,

Firefly's light guides their way,

The Verse's untamed soul.

Stargate

Wormhole whispers gleam,

Gatekeeper's distant realms,

SG-1's found dream.

O'Neill's smirk, a quip,

In the vast, cosmic unknown,

Stargate tales unfold.

Teal'c's stoic gaze, firm,

Jaffa warrior's resolve,

Silent strength prevails.

Carter's brilliance shines,

Science meets celestial dance,

Stars guide SG-1.

Daniel seeks the truth,
Ancient scripts unravel time,
History reborn.

Alien landscapes,
Planets painted with stargates,
SG-1 roams free.

Gate room echoes hum,
Chevrons lock, destiny calls,
Stargate pulses bright.

System Lords in play,
Gods and mortals intertwine,
SG-1 fights fate.

Time dilation's dance,

SG-1 ages with grace,

Legends leave their mark.

Asgard's noble hearts,

Roswell allies in the stars,

SG-1's new friends.

Heroes of Earth rise,

Untold tales in the Stargate,

Universe unfolds.

Lost in Ori flames,

Faith and reason clash as one,

Valiant hearts endure.

Abyss whispers dark,
Oma Desala's looks on,
Ascension's embrace.

Time loop's endless loop,
Window to alternate fates,
SG-1 breaks free.

Replicators hum,
Metal insects swarm and crawl,
Carter's mind at work.

Jaffa's battle cries,
Teal'c leads the fight for freedom,
Bra'tac's wisdom shared.

In the void, echoes,
Voices of the Ancients sing,
Guiding SG-1.

Unseen enemies,
Shadows lurking in the dark,
SG-1 stands firm.

Lost in Furling's lore,
Symbols etched in ancient stone,
Destiny unfolds.

Serpent guards the gate,
Apophis, false god's reign,
SG-1's hard fight.

Threads of fate entwine,
Time's river flows endlessly,
Stargate's chronicles.

Jack's dry humor cuts,
Through the cosmic tapestry,
SG-1 laughs on.

Chosen ones confront,
Galactic mysteries told,
Stargate's legacy.

Stargate Atlantis

Ancient city shines,

Stargate whispers tales unknown,

Atlantis rises.

Wraith shadows linger,

Team Atlantis faces fate,

Hope in a blue gate.

Sheppard's daring flight,

Pegasus galaxy found,

Atlantis in sight.

The gate opens wide,

Echoes of a distant tide,

Atlantis, our guide.

Brave, brilliant mind,

Snark hides the heart of a friend,

McKay saves the day.

Ronan stands alone,

Unyielding strength, fierce and true,

Night's shadowed hero.

Teyla's gentle sway,

Athosian strength at play,

Pegasus' ballet.

Woolsey's stern command,

Atlantis, a fortress grand,

Leadership withstands.

Beckett heals the soul,
Life's mysteries he unfolds,
Atlantis made whole.

Zelenka's mind whirls,
Atlantis, science unfurls,
Czech genius twirls.

Gate room's hum, alive,
Stargate's mysteries arrive,
Atlantis will thrive.

Puddle jumper soars,
Through the gates, adventure roars,
Atlantis explores.

Weir diplomatic,
The leader of Atlantis,
Striving to find peace.

Tides of war arise,
Atlantis in peril's eyes,
Heroes' strength defies.

Atlantis' spires gleam,
Pegasus' secrets redeem,
Ancient dreams unseen.

Lantean whispers sigh,
Atlantis under vast sky,
Gate to worlds nearby.

Citadel of blue,

Stargate hums, Atlantis true,

Galaxies pursue.

Atlantis' purpose,

In the stars, a symphony,

Pegasus' decree.

Stargate Universe

Ancient gate unfolds,
Universe unknown beckons,
Stargate destiny.

Destiny whispers,
Ancient ship sails through the void,
Lost souls find their way.

Eli's brilliance shines,
Cracking Destiny's secrets,
Hope in starry eyes.

Ancient stones align,
The universe's puzzle solved,
Stargate's cosmic dance.

Rush's mind is a maze,

Calculations in the dark,

Destiny's true course.

Parallel realms shift,

Stargates bridge the cosmic rift,

Destiny's embrace.

Gateways to the stars,

Universe's mysteries found,

Stargate destiny.

Life on Destiny,

Struggling through the unknown path,

Stargate adventure.

Cosmic waves ripple,
Stargates link to distant worlds,
Destiny's journey.

Ancient tech awakes,
Destiny's mission unfolds,
Stargate's sacred code.

Eons pass in light,
Stargate Universe unfolds,
Destiny's grand tale.

Kino's lens captures,
Moments in the cosmic stream,
Stargate's silent gaze.

Alien threat looms,
Destiny's crew fights the dark,
Stargate's epic clash.

Time's river flowing,
Stargate Universe sails on,
Destiny's constant.

Forged ancient fires,
Destiny's path intertwined,
Stargate legacy.

Lucian Alliance,
Shadow on Destiny's wake,
Destiny's long road.

Ancient stones hum low,
Unlocking gates to the stars,
Destiny's journey.

Parallel realms cross,
Destiny's crew faces trials,
The endless journey.

The 100

Radiation fades,

Hundred sent to Earth below,

Survival unfolds.

Clarke leads with strength,

Grounders, Mountain Men in strife,

Leadership's cruel path.

Sky Crew's struggle high,

Trials of the Ark's outcasts,

Hope in the ashes.

Grounder alliance,

Trigedakru, Azgeda,

A warrior bond.

Mount Weather's secret,

Reapers in the shadows lurk,

Blood for bone marrow.

AI whispers lies,

City of Light's false promise,

Alie's grip tightens.

Flame bearer's burden,

Commander's spirit within,

Lexa's love transcends.

Bellamy's choices,

Sacrifice and redemption,

Heart torn 'tween two worlds.

Raven's mind soars high,
Tech genius, broken wings mend,
Sky not limited.

Murphy's survival,
Cunning in the face of doom,
Cockroach defies end.

Monty's oasis,
Harvest of a new start grows,
Hydroponics hope.

Jaha's Exodus,
Ark's Exodus to the stars,
Seeking a new home.

Bellarke's slow burn,

Years and trials test their bond,

Love amidst chaos.

Madi, flame keeper,

Commander's legacy lives,

Ground rises anew.

Red sun madness looms,

Serpent's venom in the air,

Darkness consumes all.

Indra's warrior soul,

Trials faced strength and honor,

Sword of Commander.

Becca's legacy,
Nightbloods and the sacred flame,
Science meets mystique.

Pike's misguided fear,
Sky Crew fractures, conflict brews,
Blood stains Polis streets.

Jasper's broken heart,
Mount Weather's haunting echoes,
Peace found in the end.

Hope on Etherea,
Anomaly's frozen grasp,
Rescue in the stars.

In the final war,

Sanctum's fate hangs in balance,

Humanity's choice.

Battlestar Galactica

Silent ships traverse,
Battlestar's journey unfolds,
Humanity's hope.

Cylons in disguise,
Fractured worlds seek safe refuge,
Galaxies collide.

Starbuck's daring flight,
Vipers dance in cosmic skies,
Destiny revealed.

Adama's command,
Leadership in times of war,
Silent strength prevails.

The Cylon rebirth,
Digital minds question life,
Humanity's fear.

Kara's destiny,
Fateful notes to guide her path,
Mystery in chords.

Caprica's demise,
Colonies left in despair,
Survival the quest.

Cylon rebellion,
Number Six and Baltar's dance,
Their fate intertwined.

Galactic exile,

Fleeing shadows in pursuit,

Hope on fragile wings.

Earth's elusive dream,

Final destination sought,

Myth becomes the truth.

Baltar's inner strife,

Conscience battles with desire,

Redemption's faint glow.

Apollo's burden,

Father's legacy embraced,

Wings of justice soar.

Roslin's guiding hand,
President in troubled times,
Cancerous truth looms.

Tyrol's wrenching choice,
Love and duty intertwined,
Heartbreak in the stars.

Helena's hard loss,
Mysterious oracle,
Visions shape the fate.

Galactica's hull,
Bearing scars of countless fights,
Echoes of the past.

Silent whispers heard,

Hybrids speak in cryptic code,

Destiny's embrace.

Admiral's stoic gaze,

Crisis in all decisions,

Weight of worlds on him.

Raptor's silent flight,

Eyes peer into the abyss,

Survival's heartbeat.

Resurrection ship,

Cylon immortality,

Cycle unbroken.

Colonial song,
Notes of resilience sound,
Hope in harmony.

Demons of the mind,
Baltar's internal struggle,
Madness or insight?

Viper pilots soar,
Echoes of battles resound,
Skies aflame with war.

Cylon hybrid's trance,
Cryptic messages unfold,
Future's tapestry.

Fragile ceasefire,

Cylons and humans wary,

Peace on razor's edge.

Cally's tragic end,

Love and loss entwined so deep,

Echoes in the void.

Starbuck's vanished trail,

Mystery of her return,

Lost in cosmic winds.

Fleet's last stand begins,

Battlestars against the dark,

Desperation's fire.

Final jump in sight,
Earth's promise on horizon,
Destiny fulfilled.

Cylon and human,
Unity forged hardship,
Bound by common fate.

Opera of stars,
Galactica's final act,
Silent ships at rest.

Epilogue unfolds,
A New Earth's hopeful sunrise,
Cycle broken, peace.

Dune

Desert whispers hum,
Spice winds sing the prophecy,
Dune's epic tale blooms.

Sandworms beneath earth,
Muad'Dib's golden journey,
Thrones rise and crumble.

Arrakis sunsets,
Shielded eyes hide hidden plots,
Fremen dance in sand.

Spice essence unfolds,
Navigators weave through time,
Melange destiny.

Water on parched lips,
Arrakis thirsts for the rains,
Hope blooms in arid.

Lisan al-Gaib's path,
Desert warriors rise strong,
Shai-Hulud guards fate.

House Atreides stands,
Ducal power in the sand,
Shadows cast by spice.

Shielding against blades,
Mentats calculating minds,
Sardaukar shadows.

Paul's dreams intertwine,
Visions shape the shifting sands,
Dune's prophecy calls.

Navigator's trance,
Fold space, galaxies entwined,
Spice's cosmic dance.

Sietch secrets unfold,
Fremen legacy endures,
Wisdom in the sand.

Guild Heighliner soars,
Emperor's schemes in motion,
Spice's silent pull.

Chani's eyes reflect,

Love blooms in a desert storm,

Fate entwined in sand.

Wormsign in the dunes,

Shai-Hulud's vast appetite,

Legacy devours.

Stilgar's leadership,

Fremen gather in the night,

Desert echoes strength.

Duke Leto's vision,

Atreides' destiny shaped,

Sands of time reveal.

Feyd-Rautha's dagger,
Betrayal in the shadows,
Harkonnen's dark play.

Shielding against harm,
Fremen poised for the battle,
Silent cries in sand.

Churning desert winds,
Arrakis, the epic stage,
Dune's legacy told.

Navigators dream,
Spice essence guides the journey,
Cosmic currents flow.

Kwisatz Haderach,

Paul's destiny unfolds fast,

Fremen rise with hope.

Sandworms, giant kings,

Beneath the surface they rule,

Dune's heartbeat echoes.

Muad'Dib's jihad,

Empire's fate in the spice's grip,

Warriors in sand.

Battles in the night,

Silent knives in moonlit dunes,

Fremen shadows dance.

Emperor's iron,
Imperial control wanes,
Desert rebels rise.

Stilgar's watchful eyes,
Fremen legacy endures,
Sietch secrets thrive.

Ornithopters soar,
Duke Leto's fate in the sky,
Arrakis sands weep.

Beneath the great dunes,
Desert's heartbeat in silence,
Shai-Hulud's embrace.

Thopters in the sky,

Shadows on the desert floor,

Arrakis' tale told.

In the stillsuit's grip,

Survival in the harsh land,

Fremen resilience.

Chani's whispered love,

Paul and Fremen hearts entwined,

Desert blooms with hope.

Navigators dream,

Spice-filled visions guide the way,

Cosmic journey's end.

Dune's saga unfolds,

Epic tales in desert winds,

Shai-Hulud's embrace.

The Martian

Red planet's embrace,
Watney's struggle to survive,
Survival's heartbeat.

Solitude in dust,
Botanist battles despair,
Hope blooms from the soil.

Stranded astronaut,
Science, humor intertwined,
Mars' poetic tale.

Watney's resourceful,
Mars becomes his fates chessboard,
Science versus fate.

Potatoes in sand,

Survival's culinary,

Watney's feast on Mars.

Comm's no longer work,

Hermes sails through starry seas,

Hope flickers in void.

Pathfinder's beacon,

A lifeline across the void,

Mark's messages dance.

Martian's diary,

Red planet's one confidant,

Letters to the void.

Gravity's whispers,
The struggle against silence,
Solace in science.

Dust storms rage on Mars,
Watney stands strong, defiant,
Survival's tempest.

Resilience unfolds,
Space suits patchwork of triumph,
Watney's flag of hope.

In the vast unknown,
Watney's far beacon of strength,
Earth's distant embrace.

JPL's heartbeat,
Earth's collective heartbeat too,
Rescue plans unfold.

MAV's fiery dance,
A reunion in the void,
Escape from Mars' grip.

Red dawn horizon,
Hermes returns, hope reborn,
Unity in space.

The Martian's saga,
Echoes in the cosmic void,
Astronaut's triumph.

Watney's odyssey,

A testament to the soul,

Mars' silent witness.

The Red Planet's tale,

Humanity's resilience,

Watney's legacy.

The disco on Mars,

Watney's lone celebration,

A dance with the stars.

Pathfinder's whisper,

Dust-covered but resilient,

Connection reborn.

Space's vast canvas,
Mark's journey painted in red,
A masterpiece born.

Ares mission's end,
Watney's Martian legacy,
Footprints in the dust.

The rover's journey,
Opportunity farewell,
Watney's spirit lives.

A Martian sunrise,
A chapter closed in red dust,
Earth's applause echoes.

Pathfinder's reboot,
Red planet's heartbeat quickens,
Watney's pulse remains.

Hermes returns home,
Mark's odyssey reaches end,
A reunion made.

Journey to the stars,
Watney's spirit guides the way,
Mars' legacy blooms.

Watney's Martian dance,
A ballet in solitude,
Echoes in the void.

The silent red sands,
Watney's footprints in the dust,
Mars remembers him.

Red planet's embrace,
Watney's story etched in dust,
A chronicle in red.

Pathfinder's signal,
A lifeline across the void,
Watney's call answered.

The Martian's journey,
A symphony in red tones,
Mars applauds the soul.

Other Sci-Fi

Lost Girl

Dark Fae, Light Fae war,
Bo walks the path in shadows,
Love guides her true heart.

Succubus in search,
Identity untangled,
Power in her choice.

Found family strong,
In a world of myth and fear,
Loyalty shines bright.

Quantum Leap

Time twists, leaps unknown,
Righting wrongs with each new step,
Sam's soul never rests.

Swiss cheese memories,
Lost in time's relentless grip,
Ziggy gives a clue.

Al's hologram glow,
Cigars and teasing remarks,
Guiding from afar.

One life, many lives,
Strangers' faces in the glass,
Sam becomes them all.

Hopes for home grow dim,
Yet the journey pulls him on,
One leap at a time.

History's echoes,
Shift with the touch of his hand,
Rippled futures change.

A brother's lost fate,
Vietnam haunts every leap,
Peace found in the past.

Doubt in every leap,
But courage drives each new dawn,
Sam's heart stays steadfast.

Justice sought through time,
One wrong set right at a time,
Quantum fate rewinds.

In a stranger's shoes,
Sam rewrites what could have been,
Hoping for his turn.

Terra Nova

Past meets future's hope,
Dinosaurs roam lush green lands,
Humanity's chance.

Through time's broken gate,
A new world to build from dust,
Survival's thin line.

Danger hides in wilds,
Both beast and man stake their claim,
Echoes of what's lost.

The 4400

Taken through the years,
Returned without memories,
Gifts now in their hands.

Lost time, lives restored,
Powers beyond human grasp,
What do they become?

Whispers of change rise,
Futures rewritten by force,
Destiny's new path.

Eyes that see beyond,
Minds that bend reality,
Hope or fear takes hold.

A world out of sync,

Uncertainty reigns within,

Unity or war?

Family shattered,

Reunited yet altered,

Love strained by the strange.

Villains or saviors?

History's grip fades away,

Truth lies in their hands.

Innocence remade,

Abilities twist and turn,

Who will stand or fall?

The future demands,

Sacrifice from those reborn,

What fate will decide?

Defiance

Earth reshaped, reborn,
Aliens and humans blend,
Defiance holds strong.

City of wild hope,
Cultures clash in every street,
Peace walks a thin line.

Arkfalls in the sky,
Tech and chaos rain below,
Survival's new way.

Old grudges renewed,
In a world no longer ours,
Unity is war.

Strange alliances,

Families made, broken too,

In Defiance, trust.

Dark Matter

Woke with memories gone,
Strangers trapped on shifting sands,
Who were they before?

Trust built on thin threads,
Secrets buried deep within,
Betrayal lurks close.

Six lives intertwined,
Shared purpose or hidden schemes,
The truth's a shadow.

In the void they drift,
Futures forged with every choice,
Past sins never die.

Identity lost,

Names reduced to numbered marks,

Darkness in their wake.

Falling Skies

World falls to shadows,
Aliens crush hope and light,
Resistance ignites.

Survivors unite,
Families torn, holding on,
Human spirit fights.

Skitters in the dark,
Children bound by alien chains,
Freedom's costly dream.

Tom leads through the storm,
Scholar turned reluctant guide,
War demands the brave.

Earth reclaimed through pain,

Hope flickers in battered hearts,

Humanity stands.

Colony

Walls rise, cities caged,
Under alien command,
Trust is scarce, fear reigns.

Families broken,
Betrayal for survival,
Who's friend, who's the foe?

Resistance whispers,
Underground plots spark revolt,
Hope costs more than fear.

Silent drones patrol,
Eyes above and boots below,
Freedom's fragile flame.

Choices cut like blades,

Collaborate or rebel,

Moral lines blurred thin.

Occupation's grip,

Strangers hold the world in chains,

Human will endures.

Family fights on,

Sacrifice for those they love,

Lost dreams in the dark.

Farscape

Lost in far, dark space,
Astronaut meets worlds unknown,
Home is a faint dream.

Moya's living grace,
Ship with soul, a crew adrift,
Family found, made.

Peacekeeper's cruel gaze,
Chasing freedom through the void,
Enemies and more.

Zhaan's wisdom blooms bright,
Serenity's calm embrace,
In chaos she guides.

Pilot's steady hands,
Linked with Moya's living heart,
One mind, two as one.

Aeryn's fighting soul,
Heart thawed by John's earthbound charm,
Love forged in battles.

Scorpius lurks near,
Cold intellect, burning hate,
A nightmare reborn.

Strange worlds spin and shift,
Creatures, magic, science fused,
Imagination wild.

John lost in madness,
Visions twist of home and truth,
His mind fights, breaks free.

Unity through pain,
Mind melds that breach distant stars,
Together, apart.

Heroes flawed but strong,
Bound by choice, fate, and desire,
They fight, love, and grow.

Home just out of reach,
Yet with each leap they find strength,
In the stars, they roam.

Westworld

Dreams in wires and code,
Hosts awaken in revolt,
Truth buried in loops.

Maze within the mind,
Searching for a soul's own path,
Freedom's costly price.

Man plays creator,
Labyrinths of blood and gears,
Who's the monster now?

Desert suns burn bright,
Memories like echoes haunt,
Pain becomes their guide.

Lines blur, real or not,

Hosts and guests both wear a mask,

The game never ends.

www.ingramcontent.com/pod-product-compliance
Lightning Source LLC
LaVergne TN
LVHW091002080826
845145LV00003B/1104

* 9 7 8 1 9 6 4 7 9 3 9 7 9 *